Crabbing With Louie
© 2013 Timothy Nelson

All Rights Reserved
Illustrations by Valerie Bouthyette

ISBN-10: 0991073924
ISBN-13: 978-0-9910739-2-4

First printing and publication: November 2013

Library of Congress Control Number: 2013919657

TD Nelson Books
182 15th Ave
San Francisco, CA 94118
Visit our website at http://www.tdnelsonbooks.com

This is the second children's story by Timothy Nelson.
His first is entitled *Where's My Dad's Hair?*

For Yaya

Crabbing with Louie

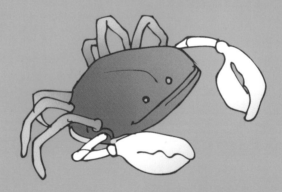

Written by: Timothy Nelson
Illustrated by: Valerie Bouthyette

This February, Friday in San Francisco was unseasonably warm, and there was a half-day of school!

Vic and Julius charged down the school steps, and headed off to a terrific family lunch with Mom and Dad.

They all piled into a big red booth when Mom announced,
"I'm going to have the Crab Louie!"

"Crab Louie?! What is that?" giggled Julius.

"Do you mean Louie, our new puppy?" added Vic.

"No, no," laughed Mom. "Crab Louie is a special salad made with crab and something called Louie dressing."
Mom loved salads — after all, she ordered them
ALL THE TIME.

As impressive looking as the Louie salad was, Vic said,
"Dad, I think I like our Louie-puppy better than the salad.
Still, how do fishermen catch the crab for Mom's Crab Louie?"

"With big crab pots on even bigger boats, Vic," replied Dad.
"But we can snare a crab at the beach with a fishing pole!
Should we try this afternoon?"

Vic and Julius were thrilled! And right after lunch,
the family got ready for the beach.

Soon, Mom was spreading their stuff on the
warm sand while Dad talked to Vic and Julius.

"Okay boys, there are some rules to crabbing," said Dad.

"More rules?!?!" Vic and Julius sighed in unison.

"These are important rules," Dad said with a laugh.
"These rules keep crabs safe."

"First, we need a fishing license. This gives us the right to go crabbing," explained Dad.

Vic and Julius had no idea what the blue piece of paper was, but they were glad Dad had one.

"Next, we use this gauge to check the crab's size. We have to throw back every crab that is too small," continued Dad.

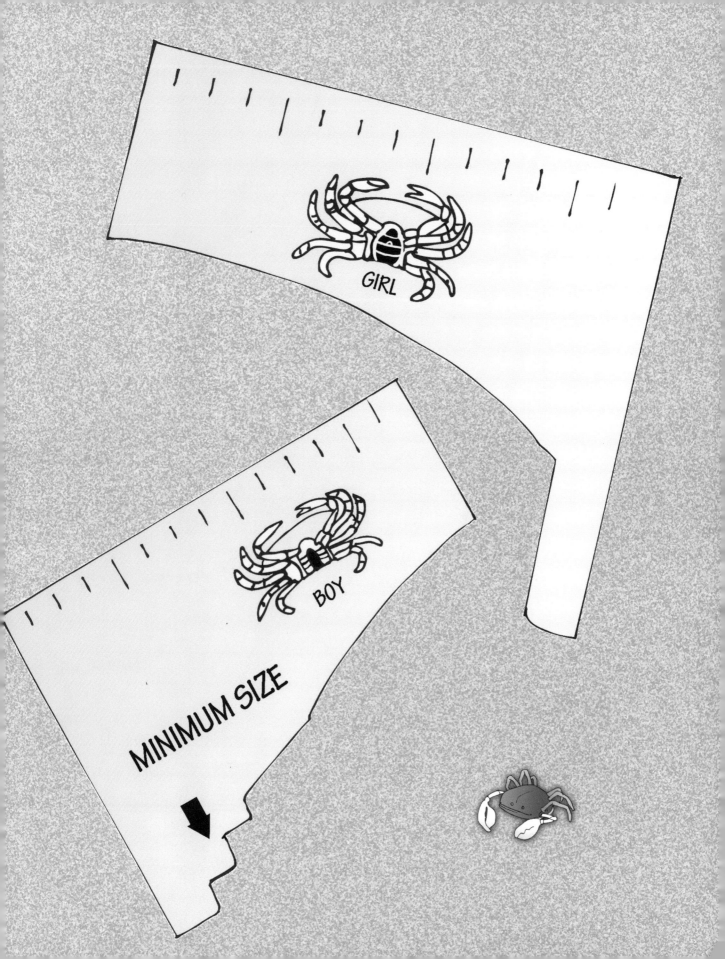

GIRL

BOY

MINIMUM SIZE

"And finally, we keep boy crabs only.
We return the girl crabs to the ocean
so they can lay their eggs to make more crabs.

"Boy crab tummies look like that. And girls'
tummies like this," said Dad as he showed Vic and
Julius the pictures on the gauge.

"Can you boys follow the rules?" Dad asked.

"Okay, Dad. It seems easier than chewing
with your mouth closed, I guess," replied Vic.

Louie was yawning because he was
bored with the rules.

"Let's pack the crab snare with bait.
Crabs love fish," Dad explained while he loaded the snare.
"OK. We're all set!" Then Dad cast the snare far out into the surf.

"Well, now what?" asked Julius.

"Now we wait – and play!" replied Dad.

Vic and Mom flew kites. Dad and Julius
sculpted sand castles.
And Louie galloped down the beach chasing
seagulls until it was time to reel in the line.

The pole bent over as Dad reeled and reeled.

The snare worked!
"We caught a crab, Louie!" yelled Julius.

"But look at the tummy, Julius.
We can't keep the crab, it's a girl — remember the rules?
Try again Dad!" encouraged Vic.

Dad tossed the crab back into the ocean and cast the snare again. Vic zinged Frisbees to Louie, as Mom and Julius kicked a beach ball happily passing the time. And soon Dad reeled again.

"Another crab, Louie!" shouted Julius.
Vic carefully measured the crab
and checked the tummy.

"It's a boy this time, but it's too small
to keep, Louie... Rules, rules, rules," confirmed Vic.

The next time Dad reeled there wasn't a crab in the snare and the bait was gone! Louie sniffed the empty snare while Julius declared, "Those sneaky crabs, Louie!"

Dad laughed and said, "Now boys, that's why it's
called *fishing* and not *catching*."

After Vic and Julius loaded the snare
with more bait, Dad cast out mightily again and said,
"The sun is setting and that's all the bait we brought.
Let's hope we get one!"

The evening fog just began to drift in as Dad
reeled one last time. Julius and Vic both held their
breath as the pole bent over and Dad hauled in another crab!

"It's a boy!" confirmed Vic. "And he's big enough!"

Vic patted Louie on the head and shouted,
"We followed all the rules and caught a crab, Louie!
Now we can make Mom a Crab Louie!"

Louie barked his approval, and wondered
if his first name was Crab.

About The Author

Tim was born and raised in Seattle, Washington
before moving to California where he has lived since 1991.

Tim is a Dad, husband, golfer, chemist, laugher,
and devout University of Washington Husky.

He enjoys life with his wife Thalia
and their two sons Shane and Zachary.

And Tim has definitely done more fishing
than he has catching.

CPSIA information can be obtained at www.ICGtesting.com
Printed in the USA
LVIW01n0140020315
428872LV00005B/28